# BETH STERN

# YODA

## THE STORY OF A CAT AND HIS KITTENS

*with* K. A. Alistir

*illustrated by* Devin Crane

ALADDIN · New York London Toronto Sydney New Delhi

# YODA was a Persian kitten.

Perky ears.

Smiling
eyes.

Pretty fur.

Long
fluffy
tail.

He used to have dreams about climbing trees,
catching mice, and becoming a supercat.

But then Yoda's owner didn't want to care for him anymore, and he was taken to an animal shelter. Every day Yoda watched as the other cats and kittens were adopted.

Monday . . .

Tuesday . . .

And on Wednesday someone even picked up Stanley, the one with the stinky breath.

There was no way anyone would ever choose *him*.

Fur so dirty it
had to be shaved.
He felt naked!

Plenty of food, yet he
never felt like eating.
He was as skinny
as a string bean.

But one Saturday a nice lady named Beth
came to the shelter and . . .

# She chose Yoda!

*What* was going on?

Had she been tricked?

Couldn't she see he wasn't as clever as Peaches or as cuddly as Maxine?

Maybe she needed glasses?

Trying to figure this out made Yoda extra tired. He closed his eyes.

**ZZZZZZ!**

When Yoda
woke up . . .

he thought he was in a dream.

Yet as amazing as his new home was, something was missing.

If only Yoda could put his paw on it.

Beth was worried.
She took Yoda to the doctor.
After he listened to Yoda's heart,
he said, "Yoda has a sad heart."

What does
that mean?

Back at home, Yoda was still feeling blue,
when all of a sudden . . .

CRASH!  MEW! MEW! MEW!
PURR! PURR! PURR!

*What's that?* he wondered.
He followed the sounds
down a long hallway.

FOSTER KITTENS INSIDE. PLEASE KEEP DOOR CLOSED AT ALL TIMES! THANK YOU!
SCRITCH!
SCRATCH!

The door opened and Beth came out.
She smiled at Yoda and waved him inside.
*Uh-oh.*
It was all beginning to sink in.
Maybe this was why she had chosen him at the shelter—someone was needed to fight off the monsters she kept locked up!
Yoda put on his bravest face and marched into the room.
Nope, no monsters.
Something worse.
*Much* worse.

# KITTENS!

Four hissing, hanging, climbing, clawing, snoring, stinking, out-of-control fur balls.

Archie smelled.

Oliver had fallen asleep.

Petunia was stuck.

Sadie
hissed.

*Meow!* These kittens needed help.
Scratch that . . . LOTS of help!

Yoda sprang into action.

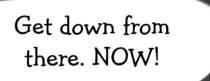

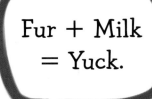

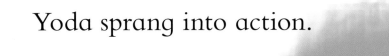

Bad news—the parakeet in the painting isn't, um, real.

Then he got down to the business of grooming Archie.

Where was this kitten born? Under a rock?

If there's one lesson every cat needs to learn, it's that bath time is an absolute must.

From that day on, Yoda spent all of his time taking care of the kittens.

They listened to him like he was their very own papa.

"Finish your breakfast, Oliver!"

"Gentle paws, Archie!"

"Use your indoor voice, Sadie!"

"No biting Archie's tail, Petunia!"

At bedtime some of the kittens even slept snuggled
under his fur.

Sadie meowed in her sleep and Oliver flexed his
claws, but Yoda had to admit he didn't really mind.

He slept with one eye open to make sure no one
got into trouble—especially Petunia.

One afternoon Yoda was teaching Archie to chew
his food bite by bite when he thought, *Wait a minute.*
His eyes scanned the room.
Oliver: Check.
Sadie: Check.
Petunia: Petunia? *Yikes!*

Yoda raced through the house.

He checked on the
kitchen counters . . .

under the living room sofa . . .

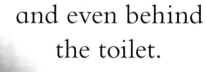

and even behind
the toilet.

He was out of breath and his heart was pounding.
Where was Petunia?

SQUEAAKKKKKKK!

She had climbed to the very
top shelf of Beth's closet and
couldn't get down!

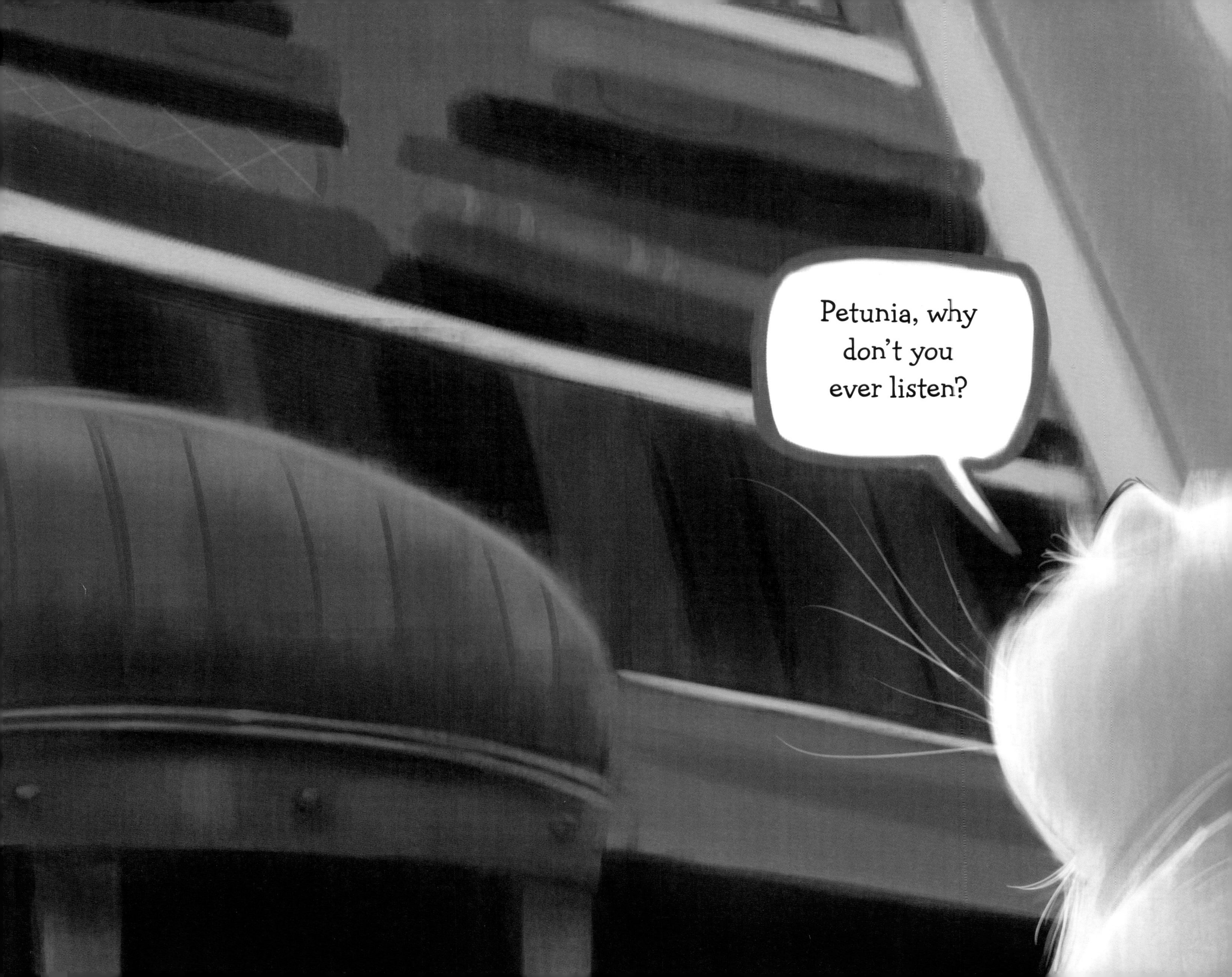
Petunia, why don't you ever listen?

Yoda was about to tell Petunia he would catch her, when she—

J-U-M-P-E-D-!

OOOOO-F!

Beth and the kittens raced into the closet. "Yoda! Oh no! Are you okay?" she asked. Yoda just blinked.

Poor Papa!

Beth was so worried she took Yoda back to the doctor.

He told her Yoda wasn't hurt one little hair, and this time when he listened to his heart, he said, "Yoda has a happy heart."

Of course, Yoda didn't understand much of what was being said.

He just wished they would cut the chitchat.

He had to get back home.

Who knew what the kittens were up to?

Petunia could be climbing the drapes.

Sadie could be attacking a school of fish on cat TV.

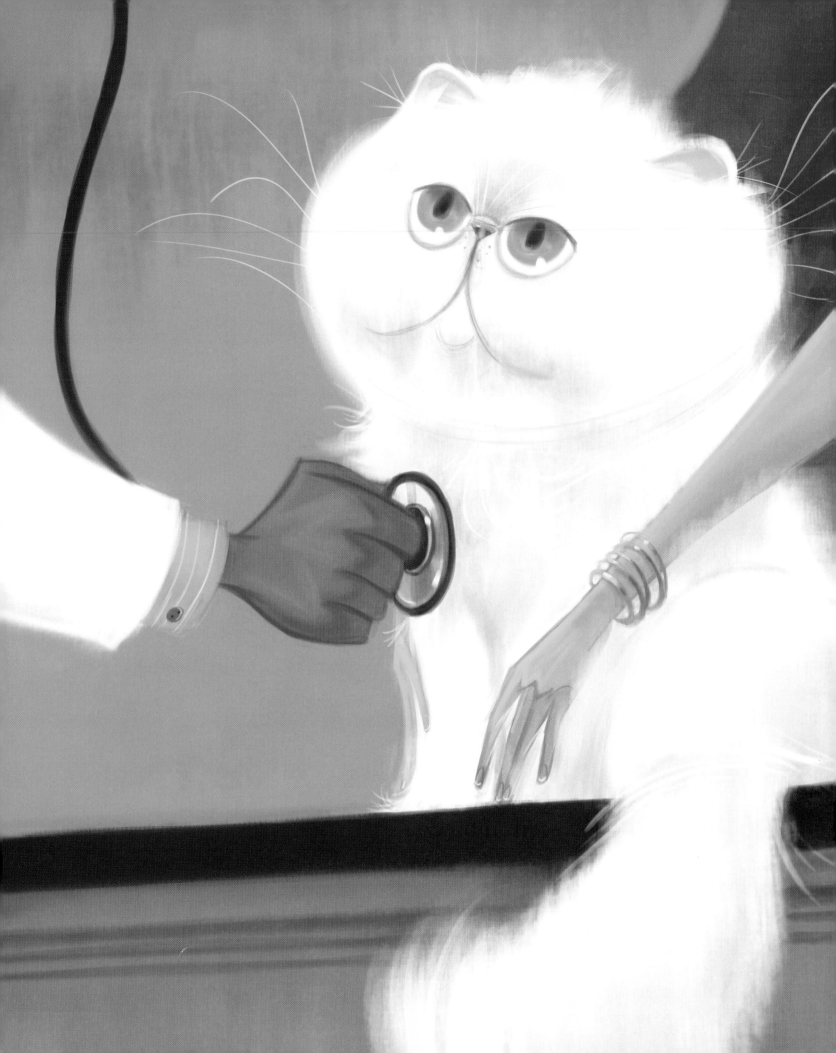

That night Yoda gobbled down his food and washed his fur, which had grown fluffy and white. Smiling at the kittens who were all sleeping around him, he caught a quick catnap.

Being a foster papa was tough work, but someone had to do it.

And Yoda had finally become the supercat he'd always imagined he could be.

*I would like to dedicate this book to everyone who adopts special-needs animals. —B.S.*

*This book is dedicated to my beautiful wife, muse, and love of my life, Whitney Crane. —D.C.*

**All the author's proceeds from this book will be donated to North Shore Animal League America's Bianca's Furry Friends campaign. To learn more about the campaign, please visit animalleague.org.**

## THE STORY BEHIND THE STORY

My love for animals is truly my passion in life. As an adopter, foster parent, and spokesperson for North Shore Animal League America, the world's largest no-kill, rescue, and adoption organization, I have experienced how adopting a pet can change your life for the better. The joy of nurturing cats and dogs and placing them into safe and wonderful homes is my bliss. I love being thanked by people for opening their eyes to adoption and saving a life. Adopting a pet is one of life's most beautiful experiences. Since we live with six adopted resident cats and have foster kittens at all times, our home is filled with so much love!

When my husband and I adopted Yoda, he was given only three to six months to live due to his failing heart. But he has surprised everyone, and is still doing great at six months and counting. His heart continues to grow stronger, and we feel it's because he has "love and purpose." Yoda is a special "kiss from Bianca," our beloved bulldog who passed away and who looks down and smiles at all of Yoda's wonderful work.

All of my proceeds from this book will be donated to North Shore Animal League America's largest expansion in history: Bianca's Furry Friends. This state-of-the-art center will consist of cage-free living for cats and increase the number of lives we can save by providing the room needed to help more puppy-mill and adult-dog rescues. To learn more about adopting and our mission to saves lives, please visit animalleague.org. Adopt from your local shelter today!

Go Yoda!!

ALADDIN An imprint of Simon & Schuster Children's Publishing Division · 1230 Avenue of the Americas, New York, New York 10020
First Aladdin hardcover edition November 2014 · Text copyright © 2014 by BiancaJane, LLC. · Illustrations copyright © 2014 by Devin Crane
All rights reserved, including the right of reproduction in whole or in part in any form.
ALADDIN is a trademark of Simon & Schuster, Inc., and related logo is a registered trademark of Simon & Schuster, Inc.
For information about special discounts for bulk purchases, please contact Simon & Schuster Special Sales at 1-866-506-1949 or business@simonandschuster.com.
The Simon & Schuster Speakers Bureau can bring authors to your live event. For more information or to book an event contact
the Simon & Schuster Speakers Bureau at 1-866-248-3049 or visit our website at www.simonspeakers.com.
Designed by Jessica Handelman · The illustrations for this book were rendered digitally. · The text of this book was set in Bembo Infant.
Manufactured in the United States of America  1014 LAK · 2  4  6  8  10  9  7  5  3  1 · This book is cataloged with the Library of Congress.
ISBN 978-1-4814-4407-1 (hc) · ISBN 978-1-4814-4408-8 (eBook)